GW00854929

HAIRY HAIRY

Story and Illustrations by
Martin Ursell

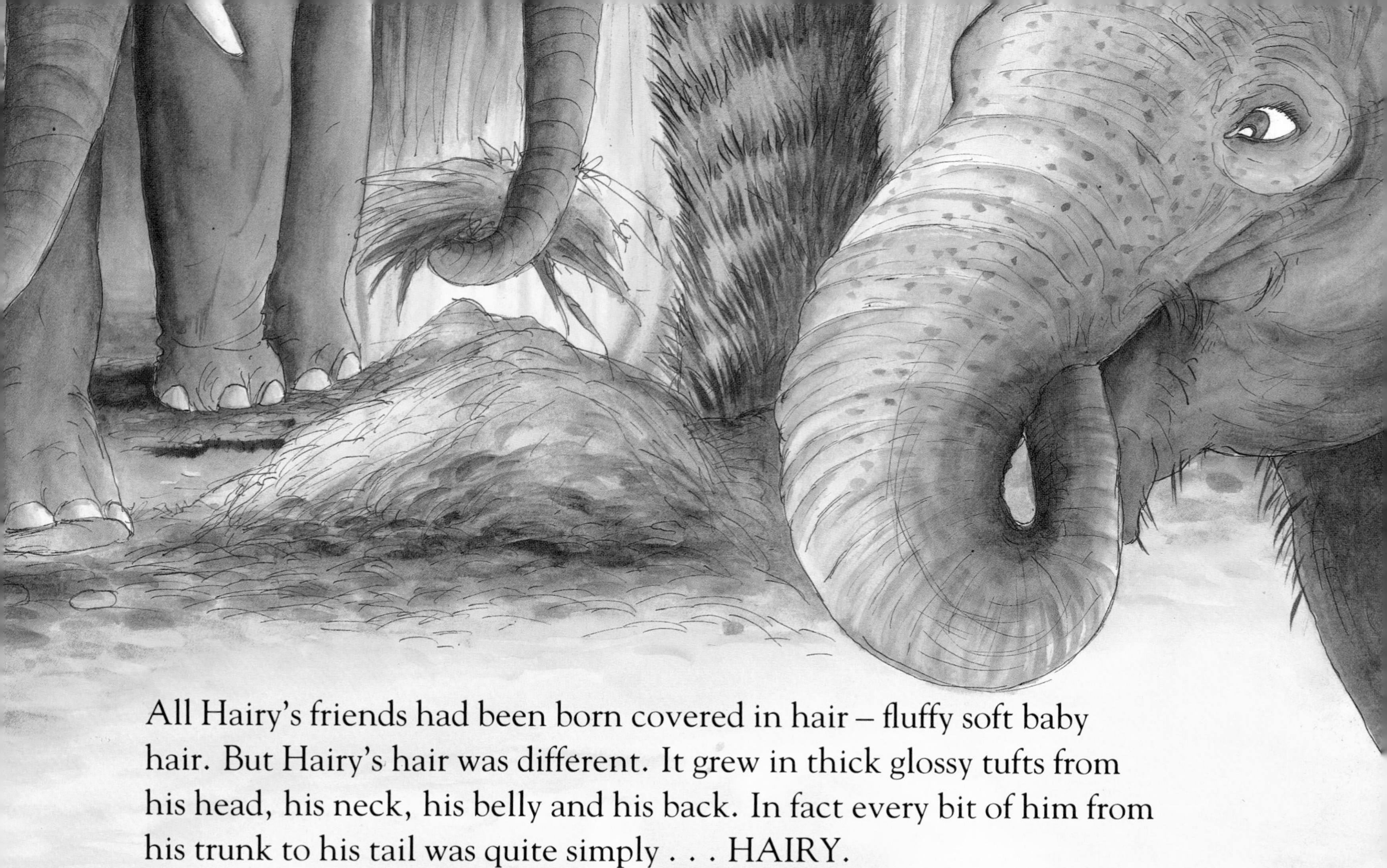

All Hairy's friends had been born covered in hair – fluffy soft baby hair. But Hairy's hair was different. It grew in thick glossy tufts from his head, his neck, his belly and his back. In fact every bit of him from his trunk to his tail was quite simply . . . HAIRY.

"I've never seen such a hairy baby," said his aunt. "Perhaps he's really a great hairy mammoth."

"Baby elephants are *meant* to be hairy," snapped his mother.

But as Hairy's birthdays came and went, he didn't get any less hairy. If anything he seemed to be getting hairier. Even his mother began to worry.

"His friends call him a silly hairy baby, now," she said. "They think they're very grown-up, just because they've all lost their baby hair."

"Most odd, dear," said Aunty. "I'd take him to see Dr Ratwhaty. He can cure most things."

"What's wrong with being hairy?" cried Hairy to his friends. "And, anyway, what could a doctor do about it?"

"Spray you with hot hair-withering lotion," suggested Twiglet. "It doesn't sting . . . much!"

"Give you a huge dose of bird-dropping oil," said Banyan.

"Shut you up in a dark cave without any food," said Teak.

"Then I expect he'll pull out each hair . . ."

Hairy didn't wait to hear any more.
He slunk soundlessly into the tall grass.
He would go to his secret hiding place and NEVER come back.

He passed within trunk's reach of
Dr Ratwhaty's surgery.

He almost stumbled over old bald
Tusker who was taking a nap in the sun.

No one saw him go, nor heard him pass.

He slipped silently through a bamboo thicket, across a river, through a ravine, and into . . . the pink king coconut grove.

"No more chewy old bamboo shoots for me," thought Hairy, giving a tree a good shake.

Down came an enormous ripe coconut, bounced on Hairy's head and split open on the rocky ground. Hairy gulped down the juice, then gobbled up the thick, sweet flesh. It was heavenly; like eating bananas, peanuts, sugar cane, and curry, all at the same time.

Hairy shook down another coconut and ate it, then another, and another, and another . . .

“Don’t worry,” said Aunty to Hairy’s mother, “he’ll be back when he gets hungry.”

But Hairy didn’t come back. He was far too happy stuffing himself with his favourite food.

His poor mother and aunt searched for him everywhere.

They looked . . .

In the tall grasses where the old bald bulls grazed;

In the bamboo thicket where the juiciest shoots grew.

Even in the deep dark caves which they knew were too scary for Hairy.

For days his friends kept watch at the water-hole.

"If only Hairy would come home . . ." said Twiglet.

"We'd never tease him again," said Banyan.

"I always wished I had spiky hair like Hairy," said Teak.

"Me too!" chorused Banyan and Twiglet.

Meanwhile, Hairy had
discovered two strange things.
He was getting hairier, and
hairier, and hairier; and . . .
he was sick of eating
pink king coconuts!

He'd also had an idea!

He found an old tin bowl into which he cracked six of the largest, ripest, juiciest, pink king coconuts. He added a few green banana leaves . . .

Next morning, just as Hairy's mother and aunty were putting up a poster, two very old elephants ambled into the clearing.

"LOST
One little elephant
answers to the name of
HAIRY
Big Reward"

"Ah, I know Hairy," said old Tusker. "What I wouldn't do to be young and hairy like him again.

"He never would tell me how he kept his hair so bushy."

"Nor me," agreed Greytusk. "But I haven't seen him for days – not since he nearly tripped over me when I was dozing down by the bamboo."

Without waiting to hear another word, Hairy's mother and aunty thundered off to the bamboo thicket. They were just in time to see Hairy emerge, looking very round, very hairy, and very pleased with himself. Hairy's mother was overjoyed!

"HAIRY, you're s . . ." *safe*, she meant to say. What she did say was, "HAIRY, you're s . . . so HAIRY! Come along. I'm taking you to see Dr Ratwhaty. Now!"

For once, Aunty was too shocked to say anything.

"Now, let me see," said
Dr Ratwhaty reaching for
an enormous purple book
all about PROBLEM HAIR.

"*Hair: hairy noses; hairy toes; dandruff, mange . . . Too little hair: tortoises . . .* Ah, here were are. *Too much hair: elephants.* Hmmmm," added the doctor, reading on silently to himself.

Hairy tried to sneak away but, this time, Aunty grabbed him by the tail.

"What do you like eating
best of all Hairy?"
asked Ratwhaty.
"That's easy," said Hairy,
"BAMBOO SHOOTS!"
"Are you sure?" said Ratwhaty,
chuckling as he turned the huge
book round for them all to read.
Too much hair: *elephants:*
Eat a king coconut that's pink and big
And you'll never need to wear a wig!

Back at the herd, everyone crowded around to hear what fearful concoction Hairy would have to take.

"Nothing!" said Hairy cheerfully.

"Nothing?" said Old Tusker.

"Nothing?" chorused Twiglet, Banyan and Teak.

"Nothing!" said Hairy. "But I do have something for you. I made it!"

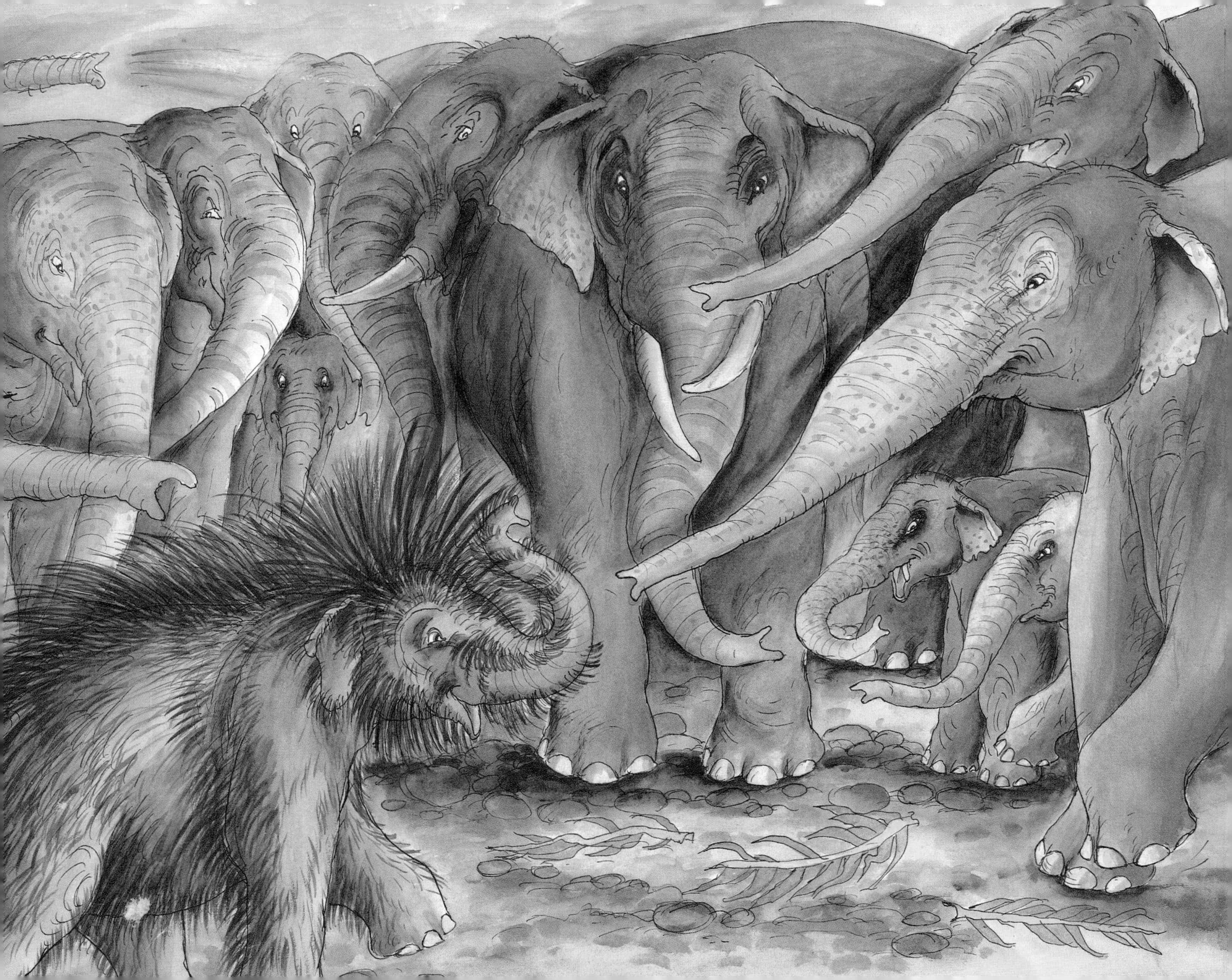

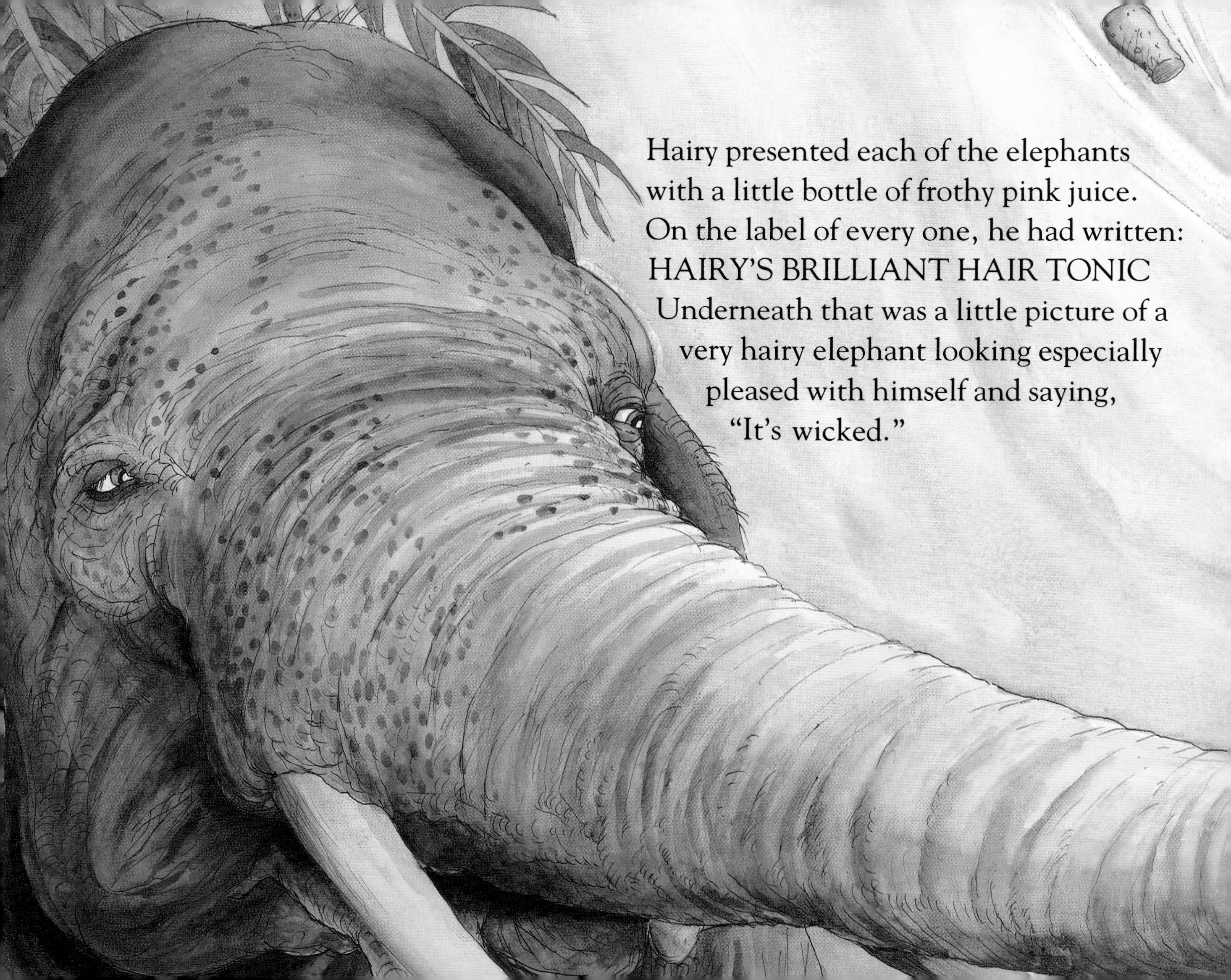

Hairy presented each of the elephants with a little bottle of frothy pink juice. On the label of every one, he had written:
HAIRY'S BRILLIANT HAIR TONIC
Underneath that was a little picture of a very hairy elephant looking especially pleased with himself and saying, "It's wicked."

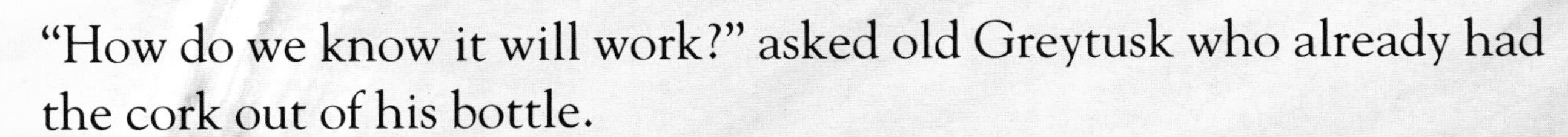

"How do we know it will work?" asked old Greytusk who already had the cork out of his bottle.

"Look at me," said Hairy. "Have you ever seen a hairier elephant?"

They all agreed they had not; and all around, corks popped from the bottles of hair tonic.

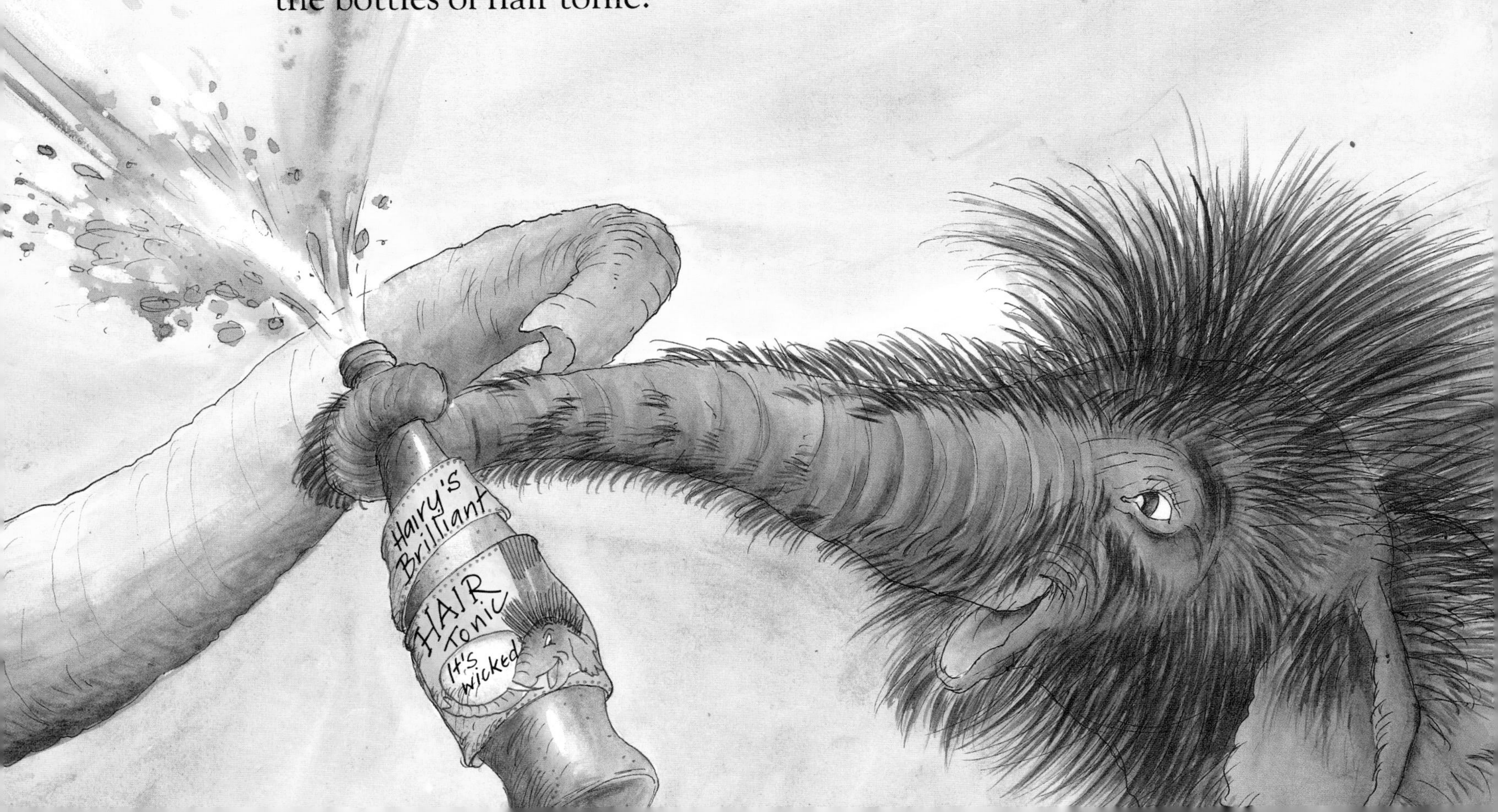

Minutes later, Twiglet, Banyan and Teak were racing about, trumpeting with excitement. Their hair was growing! Fast!

Then, very slowly, fresh new hair began to sprout all over the old, bald, bull elephants. Aunty thought they looked ridiculous, but the old elephants loved it.

"I feel years younger," trumpeted Tusker, prancing in and out of puddles . . . until he twisted his ankle.

That evening the whole herd held a party to celebrate Hairy's return. Unfortunately, some of the old elephants missed it. Unused to so much excitement, one or two of them had dozed off; Tusker had to see Dr Ratwhaty about his ankle; and Greytusk was staying in to wash his hair!

"Hurray for hairy Hairy," cheered the rest of the herd, as a garland of flowers was slipped over his head. Then the feasting began. There were pink king coconuts for everyone, and for Hairy – a large basket of fresh bamboo shoots.

For Carolyn, Roy and next-door's guinea-pig

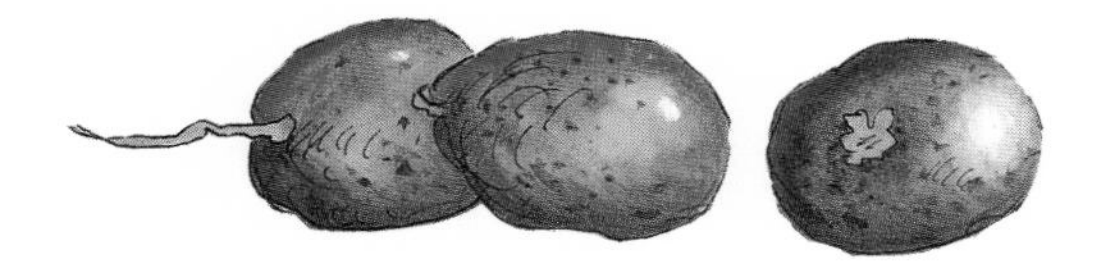

Published by BBC Books,
a division of BBC Enterprises Limited,
Woodlands, 80 Wood Lane, London W12 0TT
First published 1991

ISBN 0 563 36285 5
Typeset by Goodfellow and Egan Limited, Cambridge
Printed and bound in Belgium by Proost NV
Colour separations by Dot Gradations Limited, Chelmsford
Papercase printed in Belgium by Proost NV